Dancing Cinderella

By Katie Hammond
Illustrated by Sara Storino

Random House New York

Copyright © 2009 Disney Enterprises, Inc. All rights reserved. Published in the United States by Random House Children's Books, a division of Random House, Inc., 1745 Broadway, New York, NY 10019, and in Canada by Random House of Canada Limited, Toronto, in conjunction with Disney Enterprises, Inc. Random House and colophon are registered trademarks of Random House, Inc.

Library of Congress Control Number: 2008924680

ISBN: 978-0-7364-2560-5

www.randomhouse.com/kids/disney

MANUFACTURED IN CHINA

20 19 18 17 16 15 14

Cinderella took a break from doing the laundry to appreciate the beautiful spring day. It was so lovely, she felt as if her life was almost perfect.

Sadly, Cinderella's stepsisters never let her daydream for long.
They were always telling her to mend this or polish that. They
treated Cinderella like their maid.

Cinderella's stepmother was no better. She often forced Cinderella to scrub the floor or wash the dishes while she and the stepsisters ran off for tea or to a fancy party.

One day, Cinderella's stepmother received an invitation for everyone to go to the seaside. "How wonderful!" Cinderella said with a sigh.

"You don't think *you're* going, do you, Cinderella?" mocked her stepmother. "You'll stay home and finish your chores!"

When the day of the trip arrived, Cinderella's mouse and bird
friends tried to cheer her up.

"We'll have lots of fun here, Cinderelly," Gus and Jaq told her.

Cinderella knew that her mouse friends were right. After all, when her stepmother and stepsisters were away, she was free to sing and dance.

Before long, Cinderella was having lots of fun twirling with her broom across an imaginary dance floor.

Later, as she was dusting, Cinderella noticed a drawer on the back of an antique chest. "Hmm. I've never seen that before," she said to herself. Cinderella gently pulled the drawer open. Inside was the most beautiful hair ribbon she had ever seen!

The ribbon was soft and pink, like a perfect rose. And it was covered with jewels. Cinderella was puzzled. "This is not at all like something my stepmother would wear. I wonder how it got here?"

Cinderella ran to her room to admire her new treasure.
It seemed silly to put on such a beautiful ribbon with her
tattered clothes, but she simply couldn't resist.

As Cinderella tied the ribbon, she felt her fingertips tingle. When she looked in the mirror, she could hardly believe her eyes! She was not only wearing the delicate hair ribbon—she was also dressed in a gorgeous gown to match!

"It's magic, Cinderelly!" exclaimed Gus and Jaq.

Cinderella was so delighted, she couldn't wait to show the magical hair ribbon to her other animal friends.

At the stable, Cinderella closed her eyes and put the ribbon on again.

When Cinderella opened her eyes, she was amazed to see that the animals had turned into people! Her horse was now a dashing gentleman who bowed and said, "May I have the honor of this dance?"

And sweet Bruno the dog had become a dance instructor. "My dear, I would be honored to teach you how to waltz," he kindly offered.

Just then, Cinderella noticed that the stable had been transformed into a magnificent ballroom. And her mouse friends had become human dancers! Cinderella gasped with joy.

All afternoon, Cinderella and her handsome partner
waltzed gracefully across the floor. She had never had such fun
in her life!

The best part was that whenever Cinderella wanted to relive her dream dance, all she had to do was put on her magical hair ribbon. And before she could say "stepsister," she would once again be waltzing in her beautiful gown.

Belle handed the Beast the little book and opened it for him. On the second page, she had written: *I love seeing you smile.*

The Beast smiled his biggest, toothiest smile. Then he reached for Belle's hand and twirled her across the dance floor. . . .

"I will always miss my father, but you have been so good to me," Belle told the Beast. "Dancing and reading are my two favorite activities. But there is one more thing that will make me truly happy."

"I'll give you anything," the Beast said. "What is it?"

They walked to the dining room and sat down to eat. Everything looked delicious and was arranged just right. But the Beast seemed sad.

"Are you all right, Master?" asked Lumiere.

The Beast sighed. "I'm worried Belle will leave us one day."

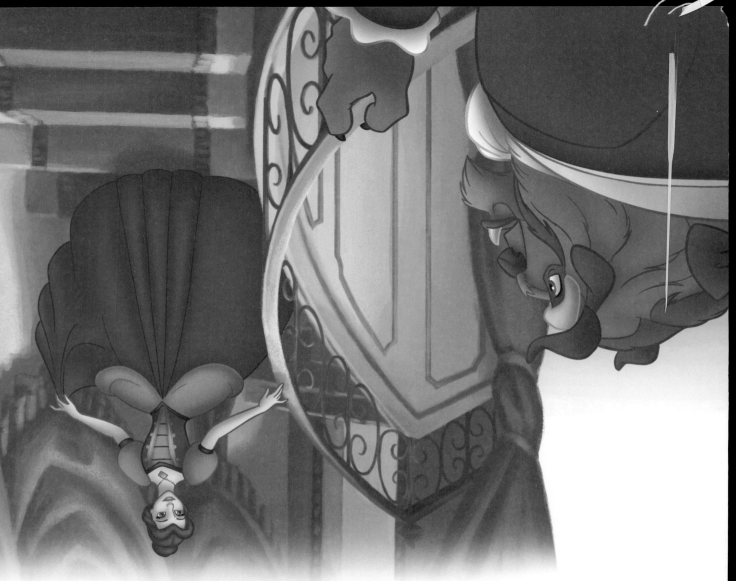

At seven o'clock the Beast greeted Belle at the foot of the stairs. "You look wonderful," he told her.

"Thank you for the necklace and the gowns," said Belle.

"They are as beautiful as you are," replied the Beast.

Once Belle had finally selected a gown, Mrs. Potts hurried to the kitchen to make sure everything was ready for dinner. Little Chip was too tired to help. He snuggled on a pile of dresses and took a nap as the others finished preparing for the special evening.

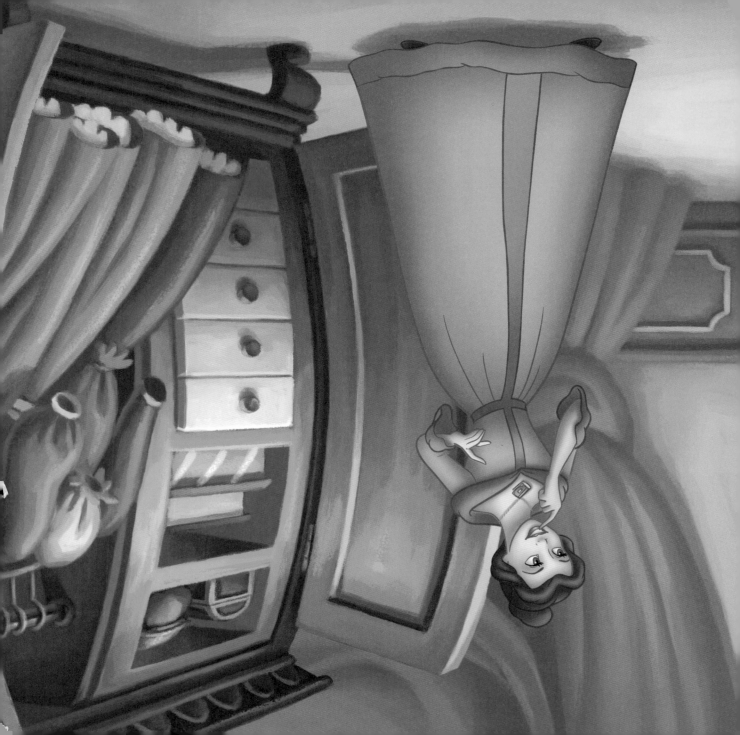

Belle ran back to her room to change into a different gown. She tried on the purple one, the yellow one, and the turquoise one. "They are all so gorgeous, I don't know how to decide."

Then the coat rack held up a deep red gown with gold trimming and puffed sleeves—and Belle's eyes lit up!

"You mean they're not from you?" Belle said, surprised.
Suddenly, she realized that the gifts must be from the Beast.
"I'd like to do something special just for him," Belle decided.
"Please ask the Beast to meet me for dinner at seven o'clock."

Belle put the necklace on, and she and Chip set off to find
Mrs. Potts and Lumiere. Belle wanted to thank them for the
lovely gifts.

"What a beautiful dress, *ma chérie*," Lumiere told Belle.
"Is it new?"

"What an interesting necklace," added Mrs. Potts. "I've never
seen anything like it."

The little book was blank except for the very first page,
which said:
    Dearest Belle,
    This is your Happiness Book. Fill it with whatever makes you
happy and wear it close to your heart.

Chip had just begun to join in the fun when he noticed something in the pocket of a green dress. "Belle, I found another surprise!" he shouted.

"It's a darling little book on a chain," Belle said as she gently turned the pages. "I wonder what kind of story is in it?"

Belle loved the way the layers of soft velvet twirled around her as she moved.

Just then, a friendly coat rack strolled in and bowed to her. "Why, thank you," Belle said to the coat rack. "I would be honored to dance with you."

Belle's dancing partner was quite graceful—especially for something made of wood!

Later, back in her room, Belle was thrilled to discover a wardrobe filled with lovely new dresses. "This blue gown reminds me of a starry night!" she exclaimed.

"Try it on!" suggested Chip.

One sunny day, the Beast was watching as Belle danced in the courtyard with Chip. It was nice to see Belle so happy. The Beast knew that living in his castle and being away from her father were hard for Belle. He wanted to make sure she danced—and smiled—as much as possible.

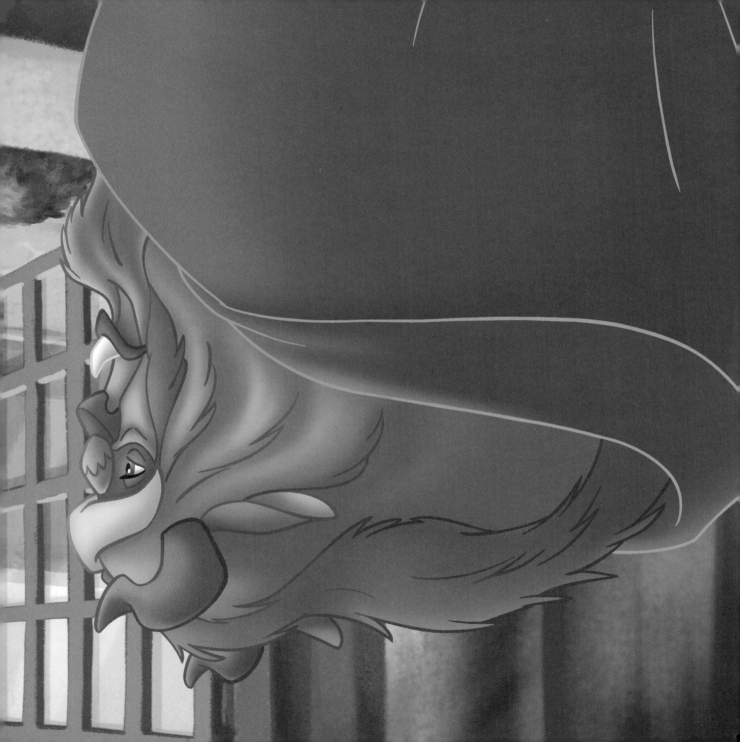

Belle of the Ball

By Andrea Posner-Sanchez
Illustrated by Dare-Kast Studio

Random House 🏠 New York

Library of Congress Control Number: 2008924680

ISBN: 978-0-7364-2560-5

www.randomhouse.com/kids/disney

MANUFACTURED IN CHINA

20 19 18 17 16 15 14